Bessie Coleman

"Brave Bessie"

was the name people gave to the young pilot Bessie Coleman back in the 1920s, when she flew as a daredevil stunt flyer in air shows all over the United States. Born in 1892, the daughter of a Native American father and an African-American mother, she grew up at a time when it was difficult for any woman to become a pilot, but for a black woman it seemed impossible. All the same, Bessie followed her dream, and in 1921 she became the first licensed black aviator in the world.

4:35

To the family of Bessie Coleman,
with admiration and respect
from another flying family
R. L.

For my darling Richard
P. P.

Grateful acknowledgment and warm thanks above all to Phil Hart, who
remembered to tell the stories, and to the memory of Professor George Bass of
Brown University, who never forgot the songs. Finally, infinite affection to my
editor and dear friend, Amy Ehrlich, who from the very beginning has
believed in the Bessie Coleman story, and in this poem. R. L.

Text copyright © 1996 by Reeve Lindbergh
Illustrations copyright © 1996 by Pamela Paparone

First edition 1996

Library of Congress Cataloging-in-Publication Data

Lindbergh, Reeve.
Nobody owns the sky : the story of "brave Bessie" Coleman / Reeve Lindbergh ;
illustrated by Pamela Paparone.—1st ed.
Summary: A rhymed telling of the life of the first African American aviator, who
dreamed of flying as a child in the cotton fields of Texas, and persevered until she
made that dream come true.
ISBN 1-56402-533-0
1. Coleman, Bessie, 1892–1926—Juvenile fiction. [1. Coleman, Bessie, 1892–1926—
Fiction. 2. Air pilots—Fiction. 3. Afro-Americans—Fiction. 4. Stories in rhyme.]
I. Paparone, Pamela, ill. II. Title.
PZ8.3.L6148Nm   1996   [E]—dc20   96-6901

10 9 8 7 6 5 4 3 2

Printed in Hong Kong

This book was typeset in Usherwood.
The pictures were done in acrylics.

Candlewick Press
2067 Massachusetts Avenue
Cambridge, Massachusetts 02140

THE STORY OF "BRAVE BESSIE" COLEMAN

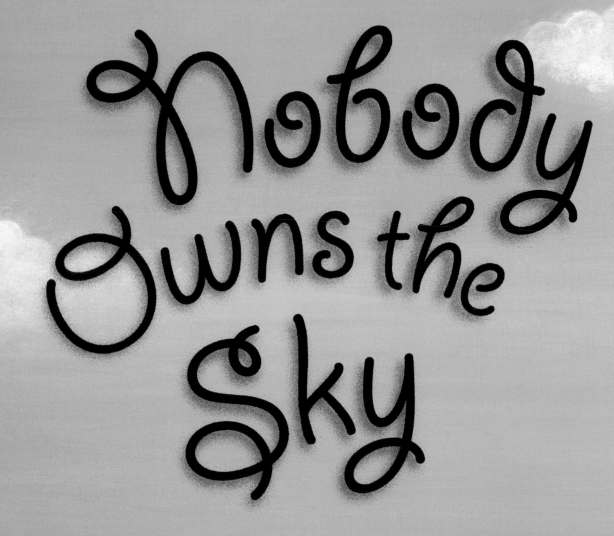

Nobody Owns the Sky

by
Reeve Lindbergh

illustrated by
Pamela Paparone

CANDLEWICK PRESS
CAMBRIDGE, MASSACHUSETTS

There was a young woman who wanted to fly,

But the people said, "Kiss *that* wish good-bye!

The sky's too big and the sky's too high,

And you never will fly, so you'd better not try."

But this woman laughed, and she just said, "Why?

Nobody owns the sky!"

Up above flew the dove, and the raven too,

With the redbirds red and the bluebirds blue

And the brown hawks circling, far and few,

And the call of the swallows that follow the dew

When the high wild geese come traveling through

With the wind on their wings, flying free, flying true.

She called to them all, and she said, "Hey, you!

I'm coming up there, too!"

Bessie Coleman grew up a century ago

In a cabin built near where the creek waters flow.

She worked picking cotton, as white as the snow,

And watched cottony clouds up above come and go.

Bessie wished she could rise up and fly, high and low,

Over Texas, a long time ago.

Bessie's mother had not learned to read or to write,

But her children were raised to be eager and bright.

Bessie worked hard at school, and she dreamed about flight.

People said she was crazy; it wouldn't be right.

"You're a girl, not a man, and you're not even white!"

But did she stop dreaming? Not quite!

She went off to college and wanted to stay,

But it cost so much money that she couldn't pay.

She moved to Chicago and worked every day

At the White Sox Barbershop, earning her way.

"White men can fly. Why can't I?" she would say,

But the flying schools turned her away.

Bessie manicured nails while the barber cut hair,

And she dreamed about flying, but didn't know where.

Then one day someone said, "Fly in France! They won't care

That you're black, and a woman." So Bessie went there.

She was young, tough, and smart, she had courage to spare,

And she took like a hawk to the air.

Bessie came home a pilot, so happy and proud

She could ride on the wind, glide and spin in a cloud,

Parachute, loop-the-loop . . . Bessie drew a huge crowd.

When she flew over airports or fields barely plowed,

Her courage and daring had everyone wowed.

"Brave Bessie!" they shouted out loud.

On the ground Bessie lectured to crowds big and small—

People gathered in church, or inside the town hall.

"Come and fly, boys and girls! Black or white, short or tall,

Come and fly, everybody! Come, answer my call—

The air has no barrier, boundary, or wall.

The blue sky has room for us all."

Bessie's life was not long, but she flew far and wide.

In Chicago she showed off a Richthofen Glide,

Her air shows in Boston left crowds starry-eyed;

But in Jacksonville, Florida, everyone cried,

Because Bessie's plane failed, and she fell, and she died.

"Farewell to Brave Bessie!" they sighed.

Other young men and women soon wanted to fly

And the people said, "Why don't you give it a try?

The sky's still big, and the sky's still high,

But you're bound to get there, by and by.

Just remember her words 'til the day you die—

'Nobody owns the sky!'"

Look above—see the dove, and the raven too,

With the redbirds red and the bluebirds blue

And the brown hawks circling, far and few,

And the call of the swallows that follow the dew

When the high wild geese come traveling through

With the wind on their wings, flying free, flying true.

You can call to them all, you can say, "Hey, you!

I'm coming up there, too!"